My Best Friend Is Jasmine

By Lisa Ann Marsoli
Illustrated by the Disney Storybook Artists

Random House 🏠 New York

Copyright © 2006 Disney Enterprises, Inc. All rights reserved. Published in the United States
by Random House Children's Books, a division of Random House, Inc., New York, in conjunction
with Disney Enterprises, Inc.
RANDOM HOUSE and the Random House colophon are registered trademarks of Random House, Inc.
Library of Congress Control Number: 2005928297
ISBN: 0-7364-2387-7
www.randomhouse.com/kids/disney
MANUFACTURED IN CHINA   10 9 8 7 6 5 4 3 2 1

The marketplace of Agrabah bustled with activity. Shoppers wandered among the food stalls deciding what to buy.

Jenna's stomach rumbled. She had no money to buy food. She looked at the hungry faces of Rafi and Salima, her younger brother and sister. "Wait for me back home," she told them. "I'll go find us something to eat."

When they clung to her skirt, Jenna gently nudged them along. "I'll be back soon. I promise!"

Jenna walked and walked, hoping to find a spare coin that had been dropped by a shopper. She walked and walked and walked. Soon she found herself near the Sultan's grand palace.

"Imagine living in a place like that!" Jenna said to herself. "You'd need a map to find your way from one room to the other!"

As she got closer, Jenna noticed an apple tree towering over the palace wall. One of its branches, heavy with fruit, nearly reached all the way to the ground.

Lunch! Jenna thought, her spirits rising.

Jenna hoisted herself onto the low-hanging branch. She quickly picked some apples and tossed them gently to the ground. Then she climbed higher and higher until she found herself at the top of the wall. Jenna could see into the palace gardens!

"It's . . . paradise!" she exclaimed. Everywhere she looked, Jenna saw exotic flowers, graceful statues, and lots of chirping birds.

A tiny parrot flew down and perched on a nearby branch. Jenna leaned over, trying to coax it onto her outstretched hand.

Suddenly, Jenna lost her balance and tumbled down into the garden. Luckily, she landed on something soft and furry—a huge tiger!

"Thank you for not catching me in your mouth!" Jenna said with a smile.

"Are you all right?" asked a friendly voice.

Jenna looked up to see a beautiful woman standing before her.

"I'm Princess Jasmine," said the woman. "I see you've met Rajah."

Jenna couldn't help staring at Jasmine's fancy clothes and jewels. "I'm Jenna," she said at last, climbing off Rajah's back.

Jenna tried to stand up, but she felt a sharp pain in her ankle.

"You're hurt!" Jasmine said. "Please come inside."

"No, thank you. I'm used to taking care of myself," Jenna replied. "I'll be fine if you just show me the way out."

"You're in no condition to go anywhere, Jenna," Jasmine insisted. "You're coming inside with me. And that's that!"

After making Jenna comfortable on a bed covered with silk pillows, the princess went to fetch the royal doctor. Jenna lay back and imagined that she was a member of the royal family. "Princess Jenna," she said out loud. "I like the sound of that!"

Suddenly, a small monkey hopped onto the bed. It was Abu. He bowed to Jenna, playing along. Jenna laughed. "A pleasure to meet you, my loyal subject," she said.

The royal doctor arrived and determined that Jenna had a twisted ankle. "She'll have to stay off it for a few days," he told Jasmine.

"But my brother and sister are waiting for me!" cried Jenna.

"They can stay here with you. Aladdin and I have plenty of room," Jasmine assured her.

"We do not accept charity," Jenna declared.

Jasmine saw the pride in Jenna's eyes. "Who said anything about charity? There's a lot of work to be done at the palace, and I could certainly use your help."

Later that day, Jenna noticed a blur of color flying by her window. As it moved closer, she saw that it was a magic carpet. And her brother and sister were riding on it!

"Wow!" shouted Rafi as he hopped off the flying rug. "That was an amazing ride!"

"And much faster than a camel!" added Salima.

Jasmine escorted the children to the royal
baths and found some clean clothes for them to
wear. When Rafi and Salima joined Jenna for
dinner that night, their big sister hardly
recognized them.

Jasmine could tell by the way Rafi and Salima ate that they were very hungry indeed.

Jenna, however, ate very little. *Once my ankle heals,* Jenna thought, *we will have to leave. It's better not to get used to all the delicious food.*

"Abu and I used to live in Agrabah Alley, too," Jenna heard Aladdin say to Rafi. "Have you ever had a run-in with old Mr. Kabali? He hates it if you even look at one of his apples unless you have money to pay for it."

Jenna couldn't believe her ears. Princess Jasmine was married to someone who used to live on the streets—someone just like her!

The next day, Jasmine asked Jenna, Salima, and Rafi to go with her to the palace menagerie. "There's something I need your help with," she told Jenna.

"Of course," replied Jenna. She was anxious to repay Jasmine for her kindness.

Animals began to gather around Jenna immediately. A giraffe nuzzled her cheek, and two baby spider monkeys settled happily on her shoulders.

"You seem to have a way with animals," Jasmine observed.

Jasmine gestured to a corner in the garden. "That baby elephant was found wandering alone with no one to care for him. We have tried to make him feel at home here, but he still seems so unhappy. Perhaps you could help," she told Jenna.

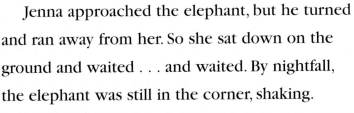

Jenna approached the elephant, but he turned and ran away from her. So she sat down on the ground and waited . . . and waited. By nightfall, the elephant was still in the corner, shaking.

From morning until night over the next two
days, Jenna stayed near the elephant, sometimes
sitting quietly, sometimes patting him, sometimes
speaking softly. On the third day, something
wonderful happened. The elephant turned,
pointed his trunk at Jenna, and showered her
with water!

"Well, hello to you, too!" Jenna exclaimed,
laughing.

After a few days, the baby elephant no longer seemed scared. He even allowed Jenna to climb on his back.

"How did you do it?" asked Jasmine.

"Well, I think this little guy was used to being on his own," explained Jenna. "It was hard for him to trust anybody at first."

Jasmine's and Jenna's eyes met for a moment. "I guess he figured out that everybody needs a friend to trust," said the princess.

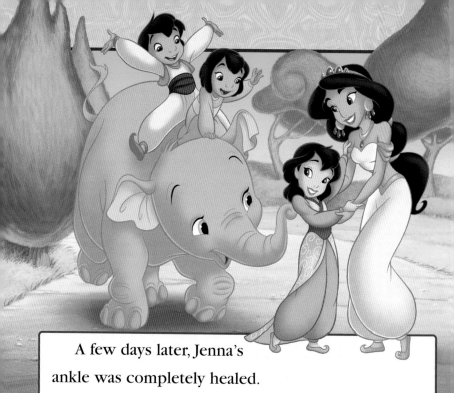

A few days later, Jenna's ankle was completely healed.

"You have been very kind," the girl said to Jasmine, "but it's time for us to go home."

"This can be your home," the princess replied. "We need someone to help care for the palace animals, and you have a special gift. Won't you stay?"

Before Jenna could answer, the baby elephant used his trunk to push her straight into Jasmine's arms. Jenna decided she could learn a thing or two about trust from Jasmine and her animal friends. "Thank you," she told Jasmine. "We would be honored to stay."